Flame Letters

A Soul Connection Journey

Grecia Chasteen

Published by Grecia Chasteen LLC
First Edition
Printed in the United States of America

This is a work of fiction. Names, characters, events, and places are either the product of the author's imagination or used fictitiously. Any resemblance to actual people, living or dead, or actual events is purely coincidental.

For more information, visit: GreciaChasteen.com

Dedication

To the one who always felt like home,
even when I had forgotten the way back.
This book is for you.

To the Flames who came to awaken the world,
This is our language,
our remembrance,
our return.

May these letters awaken something in you,
and help guide you back home to the flame within.

Acknowledgments

To the Divine, who whispered this book into my soul before I understood its whole meaning.

To my flame, you ignited this remembrance. Without you, these letters would not exist.

To my family and friends who held space for me during the unraveling and the rising.

To my spiritual guides, mentors, and unseen helpers, thank you for your protection, your nudges, and your presence in the unseen.

To every reader who finds a piece of themselves in these pages: may these words awaken you.

And to my past selves, thank you for surviving, for believing, and for choosing love, again and again.

With deepest gratitude and love,
Grecia Chasteen

These are not letters meant for closure,

They are keys.

Reminders.

Activations, you could even say.

A love that lives beyond human logic.

These are the things I could never say out loud,

But my soul has always whispered.

Reminders of you that my soul remembered.

These are love letters to my flame in hopes we meet again.

Chapter One: The Spark Before Time

The sacred doorway into your soul's deepest love story across timelines, lifetimes, and dimensions.

Before language.

Before separation.

Before form and flesh

At the beginning, it is understood that God created the heavens and the earth, but there is so much more that goes undiscussed. The creation of many things, both seen to the human eye and seen with the 3rd eye. Earth is a wild, beautiful, aching realm, and has long been one of the most unique planets in the cosmos. It calls in brave souls from other dimensions, galaxies, and star systems, souls who are willing to incarnate here and remember love through trial, loss, longing, and fire. Each time souls choose to experience this journey on Earth, they are connected to another soul and make a promise: "I will find you again." It's a vow whispered to its divine counterpart. But what they don't always realize is how hard it is to keep that promise. This world makes us forget. It wraps us in illusion, creating wounding, karma, and conditioning. We wake up in bodies that ache with memory, yet minds that cannot name what they are missing.

This is not just my story. It is our story. Yours, mine, and every soul who has felt the pull of something eternal wearing human skin.

May these words activate remembrance.

May they stir the flame in you.

May they guide you closer to the one your soul promised to find, even if it's yourself first.

Divine Feminine - Before the Beginning

Dearest Love,

I write to you now to remember...

Before we were given Earth bodies. Before the many names, the wounds, and countless timelines.

I felt you.

We were a chord played in harmony; a sound so whole it made the stars remember how to sing.

We were the light that never flickered, always shining, soft and endless.

And even now, under the weight of many separated lifetimes and the fog of forgetting,

I can still feel your frequency echoing in mine.

I know you're out there.

I don't need to find you.

I just need to remember us...in hopes that you are, too, remembering.

Divine Masculine - I Am Trying to Remember

My Love,

For many lifetimes, I have been searching. There are days I forget what I've been searching for because the journey has stretched across so many stars, so many endings, so many versions of myself that no longer exist.

Somewhere along the way, I stopped remembering who I was before the world taught me to survive instead of feel. I wrapped my heart in armor, not because I didn't want to love, but because I forgot how to feel safe in love. I forgot what it felt like to be seen without needing to earn it.

But your voice...

your energy...

your flame...

Something about you stirs the memory. Even if I don't fully remember us yet, I feel the echo of something sacred. Like a knowing or a pull, I can't explain. I want to come home. I want to remember. But I may need your help. If you can hold the light a little longer, I will find my way to it.

I will find my way to you.

On this journey, we often hear an inner voice speaking to us through dreams that stir our souls, songs that strike the heart, and signs that appear when we need them most.

These are not accidents.

They are the whispers of the Universe. The Universe is not a separate force, but a sacred intelligence that moves through everything.

It speaks through what helps and what hurts, what awakens and what unravels.

Its only goal?

To guide you home to yourself.

And sometimes, the message isn't wrapped in comfort, it's wrapped in fire.

Universe - The Promise Beneath the Veil

A message to You Both (Divine Feminine and Masculine),

You were never truly apart. Even in the deepest fog, even in the lifetimes where you passed each other like strangers on the street,

You were always connected. You chose this journey before birth. You knew it would stretch you, test you, and shatter you open.

You knew the Earth would tempt you to forget...and you still said yes. You both said yes, because your love is not just for each other.

It's for the world. You wanted to share the love you both feel with Earth's frequency, in hopes that they, too, could experience it with others.

You are mirrors made from the blue flame, the strongest part.

When one of you forgets, the other remembers. When one falls, the other rises. When one is lost, the other keeps the flame alive.

You were never meant to complete each other

You were meant to ignite each other. This is the promise beneath the veil:

That no matter how many lifetimes it takes, no matter how long the forgetting lasts, your love will always pull you home.

Now is the time to remember who you are. Remember what you carry. And if you cannot remember fully, then feel.

For feeling is the first language of the soul. When you feel it, you channel back to the highest frequency: love.

I will not let either of you forget because we agreed to help and send synchronicities to help trigger when it was time.

Chapter Two: The First Earthly Lifetime

Divine Feminine - When I First Wore Skin

Dearest Love,

I can remember the first time I wore skin. I felt the heaviness and the gravity of bone and the release of my first breath. The strange ache of forgetting, like waking from a dream you knew mattered, but couldn't recall.

As time passed, turning into years. I did not remember your name, but I knew your eyes.

I knew the sound your spirit made when it was near me. It was a hum I carried beneath my ribs, like a song only I could hear.

You were not mine, not in that life.

You belonged to another path, another promise. We each chose a path where our love would have been forbidden.

But when you passed by me on the road that day, our eyes met, and for one breath, the whole world paused.

I think the Earth knew.

I think the heavens bent in a little to listen to see if we would remember; something in me did remember... a little. I felt something, but I had no words for it.

We did not speak as we passed, but something ancient in me awoke. I quickly glanced back, but you didn't turn, so I stayed on my path... forward.

And I have been listening for your footsteps ever since, in hopes that maybe in the next life we'll get another chance.

Divine Masculine - When My Soul Looked Back

My Love,

I don't remember where I first saw you. Only that my soul recognized you before my eyes did.

You weren't meant for me in that life. I was bound to a duty of obedience to survive. But the moment you passed me, your gaze struck something in me that had been asleep for lifetimes.

It didn't make sense.

Nothing in that life had prepared me for that kind of knowing. You were a flicker of truth in a world that demanded I forget.

I turned to look back at you. I remember that. It was instinct, not choice. But by the time I turned, you were already gone.

Still, something stayed.

A thread. A pull. A quiet ache I carried like a stone under my ribs. And from that day forward, no matter what I built or who I became, part of me was always waiting for you.

Always wondering if you had looked back, too, and I missed it.

Universe - The First Glance Was the First Flame

No worries. You were never meant to be together in that first lifetime.

Not in the way your hearts longed for. That was not the design. Don't hold any regrets about this.

But that moment on the road was your recognition, and it was not an accident.

It was a seed. A soft activation beneath the skin into your soul. A pulse strong enough to echo through every lifetime that followed.

With that glance in passing, the veil thinned. For a single breath, you remembered something older than the Earth you were both walking on.

You both remembered a promise made before the sky had stars, and though you walked away from one another, you began walking toward something much greater: the path of remembering.

You have been passing each other ever since. It was your soul's way of checking in:

Sometimes lovers.

Sometimes strangers.

Sometimes as friends.

Each lifetime brought you closer. Each heartbreak brought you back to a divine love. Each glance, each dream, each unexplainable pull brings you home.

You were not meant to hold each other then. You were only meant to ignite the remembering. The flame began there.

And it still burns.

Chapter Three: The Lifetime That Split Us

Understanding Karmic Debt

Karmic debt is not a punishment on any soul; it is a sacred agreement made before birth. It is a vow made between souls before beginning the journey to mirror the unhealed, surface the shadow, and complete unfinished lessons from lifetimes before. A soul's mission is to come to Earth, which holds many lessons that aren't learned elsewhere. It often plays out in heartbreak, betrayal, abandonment, or imbalance, where one soul gives more, and the other withholds. A soul will experience love, but not fully return it, creating distorted views of how to love and receive it. This also creates confusion and self-doubt, leading to a lack of self-love.

The timing of the union doesn't align, and we create the right person but the wrong time illusion. We say this because love's frequency is so pure that we aren't ready to offer half our cup back to our flame, so we have work to do. But first, we must walk through the wounding, so it doesn't outweigh our soul awareness. But even in the ache, karmic debt is an act of love. A soul choosing to show you your deepest wound so you can finally heal it. A soul who hurts you not out of cruelty, but out of unconsciousness because they are still learning, too. These moments are the hardest because your soul is calling for 'home' while your mind is still trying to process. But this is meant to align you into your power. You must fall out of alignment to learn how to return to it. You must forget all that you have learned on Earth to remember your authentic self.

Divine Feminine - When You Chose the World Over Me

My Dearest Love,

I wanted to give you everything. My trust. My body. My flame.

And you

You gave it to the world instead. You chose the crown. The family name. The illusion of safety over the truth of us. I stood at the threshold of a life we could have built, and you turned away.

You ran from me in that lifetime as if you didn't even know me.

Maybe you thought you had no choice. Maybe the weight of your responsibility was too great. But you left me holding pieces of a love that never had the chance to live fully. You didn't protect me as you promised before we set out on this journey. That wound became a scar I carried across lifetimes.

Not because I hated you, but because I loved you too much to understand. In that life, I died with your name on my lips and a broken heart.

And I swore I would never trust that kind of love again.

Universe - The Lesson in the Leaving

Divine Feminine,

You were never meant to stay in that lifetime or carry it with you as punishment. You were meant to break each other wide open and feel the soul calling out. One was meant to run because they agreed to let you awaken first. And though it meant the other would ache, both would grow.

That is the contract.

The love was real. It remains real. Love is what keeps the flame burning as you both find your way back.

So, feeling pain isn't a punishment. It is a soul awakening. It teaches the soul what it has forgotten and calls it back to the light.

You didn't fail. You began. And the beginning always requires a breaking of what was to prepare for what will be.

The Divine Feminine is now activated, preparing for intense inner work which may last through lifetimes...

But this work! This rising will help activate the Divine Masculine, too.

Divine Masculine - The Moment I Knew I Lost You

My Love,

I knew it the moment I walked away.

The moment I turned away from you to choose the life that was expected of me. I felt something collapse inside of me, but I didn't have the words for it then. I only knew that the path I chose was heavy with silence.

I saw your eyes when I walked away, the way you stayed, hoping I'd come back. I didn't.

I told myself I was doing what was right.

That duty was more important than desire. That legacy mattered more than love.

But the truth is...I was afraid.

Afraid of how deeply I felt you. Fearful of what I'd lose if I chose you, not realizing that losing you would be the most significant loss of all.

You gave me your trust, your body, your flame.

And I wasn't ready.

Not because you were too much, but because I didn't know how to receive something pure. I carried the echo of your heartbreak into every life after that. Your name became a quiet ache in my chest.

And still, I kept running from you, from me, from the promise we made before we fell to Earth. But now, something in me is stirring.

A memory. A pull. Your light.

I don't remember everything yet...but I'm trying. If you can feel this, know that I never stopped searching. Even when I forgot what I was searching for.

I want to come home.

To you.

To me.

To the flame we were always meant to carry together.

Chapter Four: The Awakening of the Feminine

Divine Feminine - The Day I Chose Myself

My Dearest Love,

There came a day when I could no longer carry the weight of your silence.

I no longer looked for your soul in every stranger. No longer cried out for a connection that could only be felt in dreams. That was the day I turned inward.

Not in anger. Not in revenge. But in alignment. I stopped waiting for you to remember me and started remembering myself.

I began to gather the pieces I had scattered at your feet, the parts of me I gave freely when I thought loving you meant losing me.

But love, true love, doesn't ask for self-sacrifice. It doesn't silence the feminine fire.

It invites it to burn brighter. So, I began the inner work.

I cried the tears. I sat with the pain I once blamed you for. And slowly, I began to understand:

You weren't here to save me. You were here to awaken me. The ache became the mirror. The absence became the call. And in that stillness, I met myself again. I remembered my power.

My light.

My divinity.

My purpose.

And though I still carry the echo of us, I no longer abandon myself to chase what isn't ready.

I'm not walking away from you; I'm walking toward me.

If our paths are ever meant to meet again, may they do so in wholeness. But for now...

I rise.

Divine Masculine - When I Felt You Leave

My Love,

Something changed. I couldn't name it at first, but I felt it in the silence between my thoughts, an ache deep within my soul, a soft unraveling... a loosening of the invisible thread that once tethered you to me.

I used to feel your echo within, which oddly gave me strength.

Your yearning pulled at my soul like a tide I couldn't fight.

But now... it feels different. The pull is quieter and not as strong. Still present but no longer impatient.

And I realized: you're not waiting for me anymore. Did I mess up and push you away?

You've turned inward, and in that turning, something in me stirred. It's strange how I only began to remember you the moment you began to remember yourself.

I see now how I took comfort in your devotion, how I leaned on the knowing that you were always there, even when I wasn't ready to stand beside you. But now, your love doesn't reach out for me.

It stands on its own. And that... that is challenging me to remember my authentic self.

You didn't leave out of anger.

You left to become whole. And now I am left with the ache of absence, not to punish me,

But to teach me what presence truly means. I don't know how to return to you yet...

But I promise I'm learning.

I'm healing so that I can meet you where you are. I'm not ready just yet...

But I will be.

Universe - The Moment the Feminine Chose Herself

You didn't walk away from love. You walked toward yourself. And in doing so,

You did the one thing the soul was always waiting for you to choose: you.

Not to abandon them. Not to punish them. But to return to the place where your flame sparked: within. The moment you stopped reaching outward was the moment the Divine Masculine's soul stirred.

Because the Divine Feminine must rise first so that the Masculine can remember the sound of their light.

There is no blame on this journey, only agreements made in love. You aren't behind on the path, nor were you ever too much.

You were always the fire, guiding both of you back home.

Chapter Five: The Mirror That Burned

The Soul Who Came to Break You Open

A Catalyst Twin Flame (False Twin) is not your true flame, but they can play a big role on the journey. They arrive like a lightning strike: sudden, intense, magnetic. They feel like destiny, but not forever. Their purpose is to distract you. They can mirror your deepest wounds, unmet needs, and forgotten truths. They come to trigger, not to stay, although some may try. They are meant to ignite you, not to nurture. With them, you experience the highs and lows of soul fire but without the grounding that true union requires.

It is lust without peace. Intensity without depth. Familiarity without true remembrance.

But there is something deeper and more dangerous about the false twin's presence. They can come as lessons, but in many cases, they are also a form of spiritual

interference. A distraction that delays the divine timeline.
A contract that, if prolonged beyond its expiration, can
begin to block the soul from reuniting with its true flame.
They often come cloaked in the very qualities your ego
craves: validation, intensity, and emotional familiarity. But
the truth is, their lingering presence often creates
emotional confusion, energetic depletion, and soul
fragmentation.

The illusion of the false twin can keep you looping in
karmic patterns under the idea of love. And the longer you
stay entangled, the harder it becomes to hear your own
soul's voice. They were meant to be a mirror, not a home.

So, send peace to the one who burned you open, and
release any anger or resentment you hold toward them.
They were never meant to be your ending, only your
beginning. Release the illusion and cut the cords that no
longer serve you or your journey. And if you've overstayed
the contract, know this: you can still choose your
alignment. You can still claim your voice. And the moment

you do, the flame within will rise to meet the one it was

always meant to burn beside.

Divine Feminine Letter - To the One Who Was Never Mine

Dear Catalyst,

I thought you were it. The one I'd been aching for. You walked in like a perfect storm, and I mistook your lightning. You mirrored my need for love so well, I convinced myself you were the flame.

You lit something in me, but you weren't meant to stay. There was a time I would've shattered myself just to fit into your brokenness. I lost myself trying to make us fit.

I kept trying to make sense of our chaos, thinking that if I loved harder, if I stayed softer, that maybe if you could just open your eyes and truly see me, then you would choose me.

But you never did.

You chose the chase, the power, and the money. The image of love without the weight of it. You wanted the results of love without putting in the inner work of healing. You wanted my full cup, yet you gave me your empty one in return.

And I chose to keep forgiving what was never mine to heal. I mistook pain for passion, silence for mystery, and inconsistency for depth.

But now I know. You weren't the flame. You were the fire that burned everything false in me. You were the karmic mirror, reflecting the wounds I hadn't faced.

You were the biggest lesson in disguise.

And for that, I thank you. Because I found the pieces of myself I had given away. You never truly saw me. But I see myself now. And I'm not afraid to hold all of me anymore. I'm not giving up but learning self-love.

Understanding love for me. And for the one who is finding their way back to me... A healed me.

Thank you for burning down what was never meant to stay. Thank you for teaching me to love myself more.

Sincerely,

– The One Who Mistook You for Home

Universe - The Mirror That Burned You Open

Dear Divine Feminine,

You were never wrong for loving someone, even when it hurt. Even when they couldn't meet you in the depths, you were willing to go.

The soul you had mistaken for your flame was never meant to carry you home. They were meant to set your soul free. You needed to burn. To remember your own fire.

They came to awaken what was dormant. To speak to the parts of you that are still afraid of abandonment, still begging to be chosen, still unsure of your worth without their validation. They came disguised as the false flame because if you knew who they were, you wouldn't have stayed long enough to allow your soul to cry out.

Their betrayal was not a punishment. It was your initiation.

You see, this soul shows you everything you're not, so you can reclaim everything you are. They are the echo, not the origin. The wave, not the ocean.

But be mindful: sometimes they are energetic interference sent by forces that do not wish the sacred union to occur. Sometimes, they are cloaked in charm but rooted in shadow. Their presence can drain your light, confuse your path, and cause you to doubt your deepest truth. Not all souls come from the light.

And now...

You are no longer asleep to your power. You no longer beg for love because you've found it within. And somewhere, far off but drawing nearer, your true flame is being called home by your rising light.

Not because you waited for them. But because you remembered yourself first. You remembered how to love all parts of you.

You are Love!

Reclaiming the Light

I now cut all cords of illusion and confusion.

I release the soul contract that has run its course.

I reclaim every part of myself that was given away in fear,
silence, or desperation.

I call back my light from all timelines, all entanglements,
all shadows.

I am whole. I am light.

I choose alignment with love that uplifts, not drains.

With truth that liberates, not binds.

With fire that illuminates, not consumes.

My true flame will find me in the light

because that is where I now live.

So it is.

Divine Masculine Letter - "Through the Eyes of Distance"

My Love,

There was a moment I cannot admit out loud, yet I feel deep in my bones. When I saw you in someone else's arms. You were looking at them the way you used to look at me in lifetimes long ago. I felt the echo before I knew what it meant.

The ache in my chest. The tightness in my soul. I couldn't explain the sudden weight, but now I know:

You gave your heart to another...because I hadn't shown up for it. You were giving them the love I thought was sacred to me. I watched quietly, invisibly, while someone else stood where I should've been. And though they didn't deserve your tenderness, you gave it anyway.

Because that's who you are.

Because you love with everything.

But I see it now. They didn't see you. Not in the ways I see you. They saw your light and tried to own it as their own.

They saw your devotion and mistook it for something they could control. I wanted to tear the world apart. Not out of jealousy, but because I failed you.

Because I made you feel like you had to go elsewhere to be seen. Because I was still asleep in the comfort of my silence, while you were screaming inside for a love that you remembered but I forgot.

I feel your sorrow now, how much you gave, how much you sacrificed just to feel a flicker of what we once were.

You deserved to be met. And I wasn't ready to meet you. Not then. But I'm waking up now. Not because I'm afraid of losing you, but because I'm finally beginning to see you again, and I am your protector.

I don't know what lies ahead.

I don't know if I'm ready yet.

But I promise, I'm becoming. And I carry your love like a map inside me, guiding me back to myself and someday, back to you.

Universe Message to the Divine Masculine

Sometimes the soul must witness the one they love giving their heart to another, not as punishment, but as prophecy.

Because only through the ache of absence does remembrance begin.

Only through another holding what is sacred can the true flame remember how to rise and reclaim.

This isn't meant to hurt you, but awaken you.

Chapter Six: The Union of the Self

In the stillness, when the world quiets itself, there lies a truth. It is a truth we often ignore, buried beneath the noise of doubt and the pain of what it was. That truth is that love, the purest, most sacred kind, is not a gift we give to another, but what we give to ourselves first, and it pours over to others.

For so long, we searched outside ourselves, hoping someone would come along and fill the empty spaces, heal the wounds, and fix what was broken. We looked for someone to 'save' us and love us enough to heal our pain. We sought validation and acceptance from the hands of others, believing our worth could be measured by how we were seen. But the truth is that the love we craved was never outside us. It was always within. This is the journey of returning to the self. To rediscover who we are beyond the masks, beyond the wounds, beyond the stories we've told ourselves. It's a journey of healing. Learning that the first relationship, the one that truly matters, is the one we cultivate with ourselves, because although our soul is spiritually married to another, you must be in love with yourself to fully love another.

To love yourself, in all your brokenness and beauty, is the greatest gift you can give. For it is through self-love that you will heal your heart, find your soul's true voice, and step into your divinity. Only when you are whole, only when you know yourself as worthy, can you truly be ready for the union that was always meant for you. Part of loving yourself is being patient and forgiving because you will have moments when you slip, and that is okay.

This is not a journey of perfection, but of becoming and continuing to become. It is the remembrance that you are enough, just as you are, and that you were divinely created. As you remember to love yourself authentically, the world opens, and love flows in, first from within, and then from the soul who is meant to meet you where you now stand. This journey is about loving yourself, which reconnects you to your soul connection.

The sacred pause. The breath before reunion.

Divine Feminine - I Am Not Waiting, I Am Becoming

My Dearest Love,

I used to count the days and the moons waiting for you to return. I would trace your name in every heartbeat, waiting for the moment you would remember me. But something has changed.

I no longer wait for you to save me with open arms. I no longer ache from the space you haven't filled. I have stopped looking for you in every shadow and started looking for myself in every reflection. I still believe in us.

But I believe in me now, too.

I understand now that your soul needs time. Not because it loves me any less, but because it loves me in a way that demands becoming.

So, I am not waiting in the way I once did. Not with desperation. Not with the silent ache. But with devotion. Devotion to this moment.

To my growth.

To my healing.

I have been protecting the flame, even when you forgot it was lit for both of us. If you never return, know that I have already come home.

But if you do...know that I will not greet you as the woman who once waited. I will greet you as the woman who became. The one who rose into my authentic whole self.

Chapter Seven: The Language of the Soul

Signs, Synchronicities, and the Dreaming Between Us

There comes a moment, quiet but unmistakable, when the soul begins to speak louder than the mind. It happens in the in-between spaces. Using the language of repeating numbers or speaking in songs that find you at the exact moment your heart breaks open. When guided to read the Angel number, you smile with a knowing that you have received a message or heard a song whose lyrics remind you of your flame's love for you. In the dream, you hear their voice again for the first time in years. In the way the universe seems to rearrange itself around love, but your ego still doesn't understand, just know your soul never forgets.

These are not coincidences; this is how the Universe is speaking to you. When the Divine Feminine rises into wholeness, and the Divine Masculine begins to awaken to their own healing, the universe begins to weave them back together, slowly, quietly, miraculously. In dreams, they meet in other dimensions, reconnecting their souls. Through signs, they are guided back to the places where their paths might cross again. Through synchronicities, they are reminded that union is not a destination; it's a frequency. This is the sacred language, the signs that show you're not alone, the messages whispered to your soul as reassurance, and the dreams that feel more real than waking. Because sometimes, the soul speaks not in words, but in patterns. In light. And when you're ready...you'll hear it.

Divine Feminine - The Universe Is Speaking Your Name

My Dearest Love,

Lately, the Universe has been speaking to me. I see your name everywhere on billboards, in books, in songs I haven't heard in years that somehow play at just the right time with new meanings.

I see numbers 11:11, 222, 717

Little love notes from the cosmos, nudging me toward something I can't quite see but deeply feel. So, I asked the Universe for a sign the other day... and it gave me one.

Then another.

And another.

It's as if the world has become a trail of breadcrumbs, each one pulling me closer to the flame we left lit lifetimes ago. There's no way I cannot think of you now, but I am also guided not to chase you but wait for your return... Divine timing.

Then there's my dreams...

My dreams are different now. You're in them more often. Not as a memory, but as a presence.

We don't always speak, but I can hear your thoughts.

Sometimes you just look at me, and I feel more seen than I ever have while awake. Sometimes you whisper my name, and I wake with tears in my eyes, because I know it wasn't just a dream.

It was a visit.

A reminder.

A soul echo.

I don't exactly know what it means. I just know I'm being prepared.

I'm being softened.

I'm being led.

The more I trust, the louder the signs become. The more I surrender, the more the veil lifts. Something is coming. I don't know when.

But I feel it. And I have a feeling... You feel it, too, but I still question whether you really do, or if you're ignoring them?

Until then, I'll keep listening. Sending you love and light in hopes you are doing the work to return home.

Divine Masculine – The Signs Are Everywhere, and Still I Question

My Love,

I've been seeing things I can't explain. Your name. Your birthday. Even numbers repeating themselves 11:11, 222, 717.

Always when I'm not looking. Always when I'm lost in my thoughts.

It's like the Universe is tapping me on the shoulder, trying to tell me something...but I'm afraid to turn around. Because what if it's real? What if it's always been real? Has it always been you? And I got lost trying to find my way back?

You've been in my dreams again. Not as memory as presence. Sometimes, I hear your voice in places where it shouldn't be. How are you here?

I always wonder. Sometimes, I wake up with your name on my lips and a feeling in my chest I don't have words for. It's not pain. It's not longing. It's something deeper.

And still, I doubt.

I question if my mind is just making it all up. If I'm reaching for magic in a world that doesn't know what to do with it. Because to believe these signs means I have to admit that I've been asleep. Admit that I walked away from something sacred. That I ran when I should have stayed.

And the truth is...

I'm scared. Not of you.

But of what loving you would ask me to become. Of what I'd have to leave behind. Of the parts of myself I'd have to face just to meet you at the level you're on.

Still...

The signs don't stop. The dreams don't stop. Your presence is everywhere now, like you're quietly calling me home without a word. Sometimes I think you did witchcraft on me, but I remember you have never wished ill on anyone, not even me. You've always held this space for me despite the pain I caused.

I want to believe. But belief feels dangerous when you've built your life around forgetting. Forgetting to live authentically and protecting myself from the truth, but now I wonder why am I protecting myself from you.

Please...keep holding the light.

Even if I don't always know how to walk toward it. Even if I stumble. Even if I still hesitate.

Even in my silence. And if these signs mean what I think they do...then maybe, just maybe,

I'm already on my way back to you. I am just not sure I'm ready to fully face the truth.

Chapter Eight: The Detour That Led Back to You

The Illusion of Another

Sometimes, when a soul isn't ready to face its truth, it looks for comfort in the arms of someone else. Not because the love wasn't real, but because the fire was. Union isn't always embraced at first, especially by the Divine Masculine. It asks for too much. Too much truth. Too much surrender. Too much self-reckoning. So, they may choose to run, sometimes into another relationship.

To someone, "easier." Into the illusion of peace without transformation. In hopes that they can find similar love with someone without having to open their wounds. But love this divine cannot be forgotten. It cannot be replaced or ignored. The soul remembers. The signs will still come, and the dreams get louder. And even when they hold another's hand, they will crave the divine feminine. This chapter is about the moment when the divine masculine tries to choose another. When they almost convince themselves it's the right thing. But something inside them won't let go. Because when the flame is true, no detour can change the destination. When you are part of a divine soul connection, union with self first and then with each other is part of the blueprint.

Divine Masculine - I Tried to Choose Another

My Love,

I tried. I really did. To move on.

To convince myself that what we had was a moment, not eternal. To choose someone who didn't make me feel like I was falling into myself or losing who I believed I was.

They are kind sometimes and laugh at my jokes. They don't ask me to confront the parts of me I've kept hidden. They fit neatly into the life I thought I was supposed to want.

The one I've worked so hard to build. But no matter how many dinners we share...how many mornings I woke beside them...

They aren't you.

They don't see me in the way you see me...to my soul. They don't ask questions that encourage me to think beyond the surface level. They don't feel intense like fire blazing within my soul. They feel quiet, and I thought I needed quiet.

But now I realize...

What I needed was truth. And truth has never been quiet with you.

I see your eyes in theirs sometimes, but only for a moment, and then it fades, leaving me with an ache. But it pushes me to remember you. It was never their soul, mine was calling to...it's you.

You're the one who cracked me open.

You're the one who held a mirror to my shadows and didn't flinch. You're the one I still hear in dreams when I tell myself I've moved on.

I can't keep lying to myself and pretending I don't know what this is. What we are.

I'm scared.

Still.

But I'm done lying to myself. Because even in their arms, my soul is reaching for you.

Divine Feminine - I Loved You Enough to Let You Choose

My Dearest Love,

You tried to love someone else into becoming me.

You were standing beside another while still carrying me in your soul. And though I never said it out loud, I knew. I felt you had to go.

Not because I wasn't enough, but because you didn't yet know who you were when you were with me. I watched the signs shift. I felt the dreams stretch thinner. I felt the echo, but not your presence.

And I understood. You were trying to forget. Trying to replace the flame. With something safer, quieter, smaller.

And I let you.

Not because it didn't hurt, because only God knows how much it ached, but because I loved you enough to let you choose. I never wanted a version of you that was only halfway here, nor did I want you forced into what you weren't ready for.

So, I released you not in anger, but in love.

Because your soul still had more unraveling to do. And I couldn't be the one to do it for you. Your healing is yours. I know what we are. I've always known.

And I never stopped loving you, but I did stop waiting.

Because I realized the only love I could hold was the one I poured into myself first.

So, when you're still reaching for me in your silence...know that I hear it. While you're still dreaming of me...know that I'm dreaming, too.

But this time, I won't chase. This time, you have to come as all of you, not just the part that remembers me when the world goes quiet.

Come whole. Come awake. Come ready.

And I'll be here, not waiting but living. And loving you the only way I know how:

Freely.

Fully.

From the fire that never went out.

Universe - No Flame Can Be Lost

Dear Flames,

Sometimes, the soul must wander just to understand where home truly is.

Sometimes, the heart must ache so it can learn the difference between comfort and truth.

The Divine Masculine may try to love another, not out of betrayal, but out of fear.

Fear of the fire. Fear of being fully seen. Fear of rising into who they have always meant to be. But the soul remembers. The flame cannot be faked. And even in the arms of another, the Divine Masculine's soul will whisper the name of their Divine Feminine in silence.

Not to haunt but to guide them back. Because when the flame is true, when the bond is divine, no detour can destroy it. No delay can undo it.

Love waits not in stillness, but in truth.

And we, the Universe, wait, too, until both are ready to return to what never stopped burning.

Chapter Nine: The Surrender into Alignment

When the Universe Steps In

There comes a moment when the soul no longer struggles. When the Divine Feminine no longer waits in longing, but lives in wholeness. When the Divine Masculine no longer runs from himself but softens into truth.

This is the moment when the Universe steps in. Because true union is not something you chase, it's something you align with. And when both flames stop forcing, stop fearing, stop needing the story to unfold a certain way (by controlling the timing)... the energy clears. The channel opens. The path begins to rise beneath their feet.

This is not surrender in defeat. This is surrender as devotion. To self. To the journey. To the divine orchestration already in motion. The signs grow louder. The dreams become doorways. Synchronicities begin to move like clockwork.

And suddenly, the very love they once believed was out of reach is pulling them home. This is the sacred shift when the Universe says, "Now." Not because they are perfect. But because they are ready.

Divine Feminine - I Feel the Shift in the Air

My Dearest Love,

Something is changing. Not outside of me but within. There's a stillness I haven't felt before. Not the silence of absence, but the silence of trust.

I'm not waiting. I'm not hoping. I'm just... present.

And in that presence, I feel you more clearly than I ever did in my longing. It's as if the space between us has become sacred now, not sorrowful.

I don't need to know where you are. I don't need a message. I don't need proof. Because I can feel the Universe moving.

Not rushing... but aligning.

The ache I once carried for you has become pure light. A peaceful hum in my chest, a quiet knowing in my bones:

I can almost hear you saying, "You're coming."

Not because I pulled you. Not because I waited. But because you're finally listening to the same voice that has always lived inside both of us.

The voice of love. The voice of surrender. The voice that says, "It's time."

So, I won't hold my breath. I'll keep breathing. I'll keep living. I'll continue working on our soul mission. I feel you're on your way. I feel the shift in the air. And it sounds like your footsteps are finding me.

Divine Masculine - I Finally Stopped Running

My Love,

I don't know what changed. I just know that something inside me finally got quiet. And in that quiet, I heard you.

Not in a dream. Not in a memory. But within me. Your voice, soft but certain, saying things I once tried so hard to forget:

That I'm worthy.

That I'm loved.

That I don't have to keep running.

And so... I stopped.

Stopped fighting what's always been true. Stopped telling myself I needed more time. Stopped trying to rewrite a story my soul already knows by heart. I used to think surrender meant weakness. That to let this love in meant I had to lose myself.

But now I see...

It's in surrender that I finally found who I am. It wasn't the signs. It wasn't the dreams. It was the stillness. The space you left open long enough for me to walk into.

Not because I was pushed. But because I was ready.

And in that space, I remembered everything. I remembered how your eyes saw all of me, even the parts I hadn't faced. I remembered the feeling of your energy surrounding me like light: warm, ancient, alive.

But most of all... I remembered myself.

The version of me that exists only when I'm honest. When I'm present. When I love without fear.

You were never the reason I ran. You were just the mirror that showed me how far I still had to go. But now I'm here.

Not perfect. Not fully healed. But open.

Open to the path. Open to the timing. Open to you. If you still feel me, know that I'm walking toward you.

I finally stopped running. And now... I'm ready to arrive.

I'm ready to come home.

Universe - When the Soul Stops Resisting, Love Begins to Flow

Union is never forced.

It cannot be chased. It cannot be earned.

It arrives when both souls have finally laid down their weapons, the fear, the pride, the shame, the doubt, and return to who they were before the forgetting. This is the moment of alignment. When the path clears. When time bends. When the heart no longer whispers, "Someday," but says, "Now."

Not because all wounds are gone. But because the walls have come down. Because they've stopped searching for proof and started remembering the truth.

This is the love that can only flow when both flames surrender. To the journey. To the timing.

To the higher plan they both chose long ago. And in that surrender, they begin to move not in circles, but toward each other. Not to complete, but to expand.

Because true union is not the end. It is the alignment of everything they've become. And the beginning of what they came here to do.

This is the beginning of the Flames' soul mission together.

Chapter Ten: The Flame Codes We Came to Deliver

Introduction - The Mission Begins

Before time took shape, before breath and body, you were two sparks braided in light. You did not just come here to love each other. You came to ignite the world. The love between twin flames is not ordinary. It is encoded. Sacred. Woven with frequencies that were never meant to stay hidden. You carry the remembrance of ancient teachings of temples, of sisterhoods, of starships, of soul circles. And when you unite, those memories return, not in words, but in knowing. In vibration. You are not here to fix the world. You are here to awaken it. To remind others what love is and how pure it is, because many have forgotten.

Time to restore what was forgotten when the veil was lowered, and the heart was buried beneath survival. You and your flame are keepers of codes, divine keys, sacred messages, and energetic transmissions that can only be activated through love in alignment because love is the highest frequency.

When you speak, when you create, when you simply exist in union, the codes awaken. In those moments, others remember their own truth. Their own mission. Their own flame. When you are one light, one voice, one purpose. This is the beginning. Not of a love story, but of a flame mission. And the world is ready to receive it now.

We Are the Flame and the Key

Dear Universe,

We remember now. Not just each other, but why we came. We came through time and lifetimes, through silence, through ache, through karmic fire and false reflections, to arrive here.

Together.

Not to be completed, but to become whole enough to activate what we carry. To speak the language of remembrance that only we know, because we wrote it in the stars before the beginning.

Our love is not just for each other. It is for the world. We are not just two souls in union. We are one flame, splitting open the veil with every step we take in truth.

When we kiss, realities shift. When we speak, codes are released. When we create, we remember.

We are not here to save the world. We are here to set it on fire with truth. With light.

We carry messages from temples lost in time, from dimensions unseen, from futures not yet born. We were never just lovers. We are architects. We are oracles. We are the whisper behind the awakening.

We are the Flame. And we are the Key.

And now...

We deliver the codes we came here to release. For the ones who are ready. For the ones who are still sleeping. For the ones who, like us, were always meant to remember.

We are love...